A Grouch's Christmas

By Michaela Muntean • Illustrated by Tom Leigh

A SESAME STREET / MERRIGOLD PRESS BOOK

Published by Merrigold Press in conjunction with Children's Television Workshop

It was the day before Christmas and Elmo was helping his mother make Christmas cookies. Elmo watched his mother roll the dough out on the countertop. Then he cut out shapes in the dough with cookie cutters and sprinkled them with colored sugar.

Elmo stood in front of the oven door and watched as the cookies turned golden brown.

When the cookies came out of the oven, Elmo's mother said, "You may try one, Elmo. But we have to save the rest for our Christmas guests. This year you are big enough to pass the plate of cookies yourself."

"Okay, Mommy! And Elmo will tell everyone that Elmo helped make them!"

Elmo picked out a reindeer-shaped cookie. "Mmmm…these are good! Cookie Monster will love them."

As Elmo's mother was putting away the flour and sugar, she glanced out the kitchen window and said, "Look, Elmo! It's snowing!"

"Oh, boy! Mommy, may Elmo please go outside to play?"

"Yes, dear. Let's put on your coat and boots. Here is a big scarf to tie around your neck. Keep dry and don't stay out too long."

"Okay, Mommy!"

And Elmo ran out the door and down Sesame Street
to build a snowmonster. He saw the footprints that his
boots made in the new snow.

The snow was as white and fine as the flour Elmo's
mother sprinkled on the counter for the cookie dough.
Snowflakes drifted down and clung to Elmo's hat and
scarf. He opened his mouth to catch some more.

All along Sesame Street, Elmo saw his friends getting
ready for Christmas. Ernie and Bert were carrying a
Christmas tree. Luis was stringing colored lights in the
window of the Fix-It Shop. Big Bird was decorating a
little Christmas tree. Herry Monster had dressed up
like Santa Claus, and he was ringing a bell and
collecting toys and food for needy families. The Count
was counting snowflakes as they fell.

"One beautiful snowflake! Two beautiful snowflakes!
Three, four, five, six, seven, eight…so many beautiful
snowflakes! Wonderful!"

"Merry Christmas, everybody!" Elmo shouted.

"Merry Christmas, Elmo!" his friends called back.

Elmo passed by Oscar's trash can. "Merry Christmas, Oscar!"

"Humph! I hate Christmas!" said Oscar.

Elmo stopped suddenly. He lifted up the earflaps of his cap and said, "Would you please say that again, Oscar? Elmo doesn't think he heard right."

"Of course I will. I'll say it again and again and again. I hate Christmas. I hate Christmas. I hate Christmas!"

"But how could you hate Christmas, Oscar? There's nothing about Christmas to hate!"

"Oh, yes there is. There's all that ho-ho-ho-ing and fa-la-la-ing. There's everyone going around smiling and being cheerful and giving each other nice presents. This is the worst time of the year for grouches."

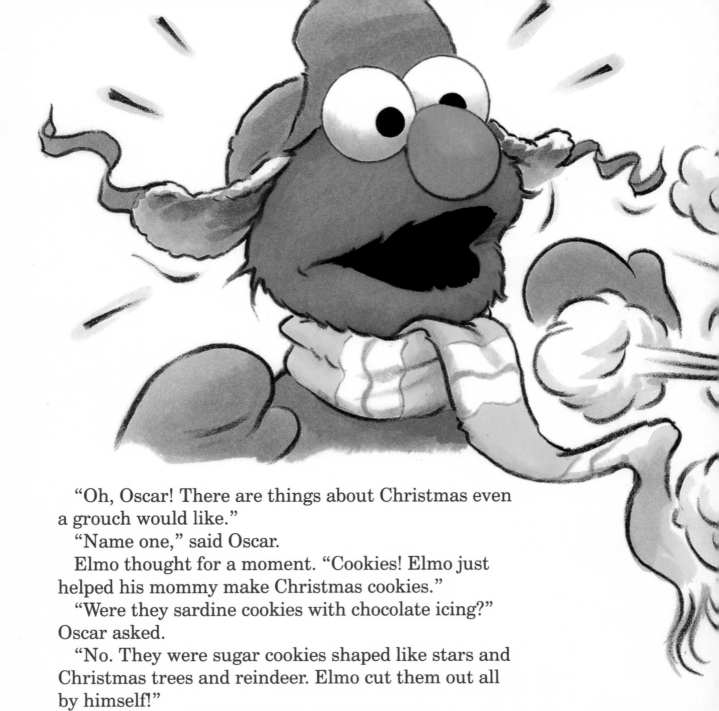

"Oh, Oscar! There are things about Christmas even a grouch would like."

"Name one," said Oscar.

Elmo thought for a moment. "Cookies! Elmo just helped his mommy make Christmas cookies."

"Were they sardine cookies with chocolate icing?" Oscar asked.

"No. They were sugar cookies shaped like stars and Christmas trees and reindeer. Elmo cut them out all by himself!"

Oscar scowled. "Yucch! They sound awful!"

"Just wait, Oscar! Elmo will be right back! Elmo is going to find a *zillion* reasons for Oscar to like Christmas!"

"Don't worry. I'm not going anywhere until the holidays are over!" grumbled Oscar. And he disappeared inside his trash can and slammed the lid down with a crash.

Elmo forgot all about building snowmonsters. He went looking for reasons for Oscar to like Christmas. If he couldn't find a zillion, he was sure he could find a few.

First Elmo stopped at Big Bird's nest. Elmo told him what he wanted to do. Big Bird said, "I've got an idea! I'll meet you at Oscar's trash can in one hour."

Next Elmo stopped to visit Ernie and Bert. They said they'd help, too. Elmo stopped to see Herry and then The Count. They all agreed to meet at Oscar's.

Elmo raced back home and told his mother what he
wanted to do.

"That sounds disgusting," she said. But she helped
anyway.

When everything was ready, Elmo hurried to Oscar's can.
His friends were there, just as they had promised.

"Merry Christmas, Oscar!" Elmo called as he knocked on
the trash can lid.

Oscar popped out of his can. "I told you, I hate Christmas!"

Elmo laughed. "And Elmo told *you* he was going to find a
zillion reasons why you would like it."

"So, did you?" Oscar asked.

"No, Oscar. But Elmo found a few really good ones!"

Ernie and Bert handed Oscar a little Christmas tree.
It was decorated with old tin cans, orange peels, and
bits of raggedy string.

"That's not a bad-looking Christmas tree. You guys
decorated it just for me, huh?"

"See, Oscar," said Elmo. "That's one thing to like
about Christmas!"

"Well, thanks, you guys."

"I like Christmas because it's a time for families to get together." said Big Bird. "Tomorrow my Granny Bird is coming to visit."

"So?"

"So, maybe Grundgetta would come and visit you if you invited her, Oscar," suggested Big Bird.

"Hmmm...." said Oscar. "That's not the worst idea I've ever heard. Grundgetta and I could sit around complaining and grumbling."

"You see? That's *another* nice thing about Christmas — it's a time for families to enjoy themselves," said Big Bird.

Herry said, "I like Christmas because it's about sharing and helping others. Today I collected toys and food for families who need them. Tonight Grover and I are going to deliver them. You don't happen to have anything to share, do you, Oscar?"

"Just a minute." Oscar disappeared into his trash can.

He came back a few seconds later. "Here. Maybe someone could use this," said Oscar, as he handed Herry a brand-new, red-and-white-striped scarf.

"Why, thank you, Oscar!" said Herry. "I'm sure someone could use it. Doesn't it feel good to help someone else?"

"I suppose so. It sure feels good to get rid of that scarf. It's too clean and it doesn't have one moth hole in it. I wouldn't want Grundgetta to see it if she comes tomorrow."

"Oscar, Elmo made twelve reasons for you to like Christmas!" said Elmo, "Here are a dozen sardine Christmas cookies with chocolate icing. Merry Christmas, Oscar!"

"There is something else to like about Christmas,"
said The Count.

"What's that?" asked Oscar.

"Your friends! When you count your blessings, count
your friends. Let me count them for you… one
friend… two friends…"

"Never mind, Count! I can do it," said Oscar.

Oscar was quiet for a minute. Finally he turned to
Elmo and said, "Okay, I give up! You were right, Elmo.
Christmas isn't so bad after all."

Then Oscar took a bite of a sardine cookie. "And
these cookies are delicious. Thanks, Elmo. And,
Merry Christmas."

Then everybody began to sing, and Oscar sang the